Giant Island

Written by Jane Yolen   Illustrated by Doug Keith

FLASHLIGHT PRESS

FX: 7-22

For Shari. She knows why! –JY

To Beth and Corie Lyn, a "giant" hug
for your love and support! –DK

Copyright © 2022 by Flashlight Press • Text copyright © 2022 by Jane Yolen • Concept and illustrations copyright © 2022 by Doug Keith
First Edition – August 2022.
Library of Congress Control Number: 2021951768.
Hardcover 9781947277182 • eBook editions 9781947277199
Editor: Shari Dash Greenspan • Graphic Design: The Virtual Paintbrush
This book was typeset in Garamond. The illustrations were rendered traditionally using gouache and colored pencil on cold press illustration board.
Distributed by IPG • ipgbook.com
Flashlight Press • 527 Empire Blvd. • Brooklyn, NY 11225 • FlashlightPress.com

Giant Island sat low in the water as the boat approached.

"Why is it called Giant Island?" Ava asked, looking at the map.

"Always been Giant Island," Grandpa said, shifting gears. "That's what my grandpa told me. We came here to fish when I was your age."

"But it's so small," Mason said. "No giant could live here."

Cooper barked.

"Maybe giant fish live here," Grandpa said as he collected his gear.

"Or maybe a tiny giant," Ava joked.

Cooper barked again and Mason laughed. "Let's grab those tall sticks and look for giants!" he said.

"Look all you want," Grandpa said. "I've got fish to catch."

"Sure, Grandpa," Ava teased. "Giant fish."

Cooper ran ahead, barking loudly.

"Hey!" Mason said. "Cooper found some steps!"

They discovered a cave dripping with mystery…

found creatures creeping and crawling through history...

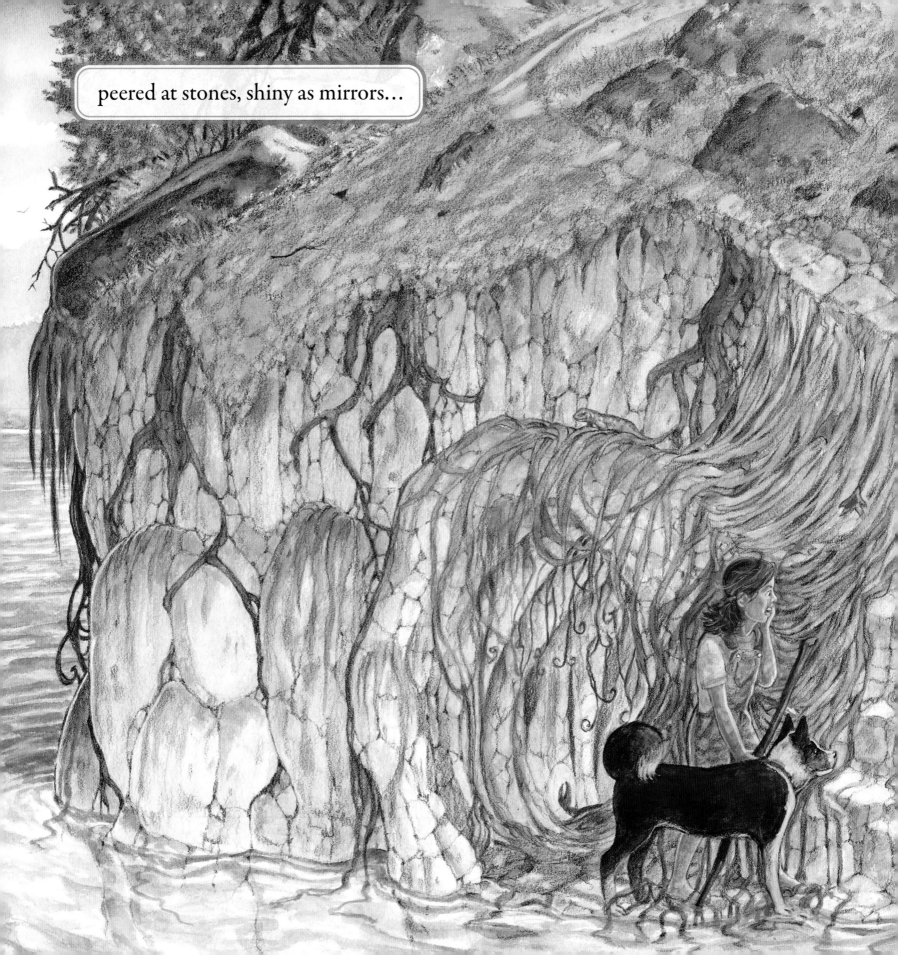

peered at stones, shiny as mirrors…

and leaped into water bubbling with secrets –

and brimming with surprises.

There seemed to be magic everywhere.

"No giant on this island," said Ava, climbing onto a rocky ledge.

"No giant," Mason agreed, running after Cooper.

No giant?

Cooper turned and barked.

NO GIANT?

Cooper barked as loud as thunder, and Ava understood. "Mason, look! The whole island is a giant!"

Mason looked – and grinned a giant grin.

"Time to go," Grandpa called as the kids returned to the island. "Haven't caught a thing. Something's disturbing the fish."

"We know," Mason said.

Ava giggled.

"Know what?"
asked Grandpa,
starting the engine.
"Know what was
disturbing the fish,"
Mason said.
"And we know
why it's called Giant
Island," Ava added.

"There IS a giant, Grandpa," Mason said.

"A huge giant," Ava said, "who wanted to play with us!"

"Is that so," Grandpa said.

"Goodbye, Giant," Ava called.
"We'll be back!" Mason added.
Cooper barked a goodbye.
Grandpa chuckled and peeked over the kids' heads. "Imagine – talking to an island," he said.

Then Grandpa shifted into high gear and whispered, "Always good to see you, old friend."

The kids couldn't hear Grandpa, but the giant heard every word – and grinned a giant grin.